ERIC CARLE

Have You Seen My Cat?

WITHDRAWN

by Eric Carle

READY-TO-READ

SIMON SPOTLIGHT

New York   London   Toronto   Sydney   New Delhi

Dedicated to
all the cats in my life

SIMON SPOTLIGHT

An imprint of Simon & Schuster Children's Publishing Division

1230 Avenue of the Americas, New York, New York 10020

Copyright © 1987 by Eric Carle Corp.

First Simon Spotlight Ready-to-Read edition 2012

For information about special discounts for bulk purchases, please contact Simon & Schuster Special Sales at 1-866-506-1949 or business@simonandschuster.com.

The Simon & Schuster Speakers Bureau can bring authors to your live event. For more information or to book an event contact the Simon & Schuster Speakers Bureau at 1-866-248-3049 or visit our website at www.simonspeakers.com.

Manufactured in the United States of America 0312 LAK

First Edition 10 9 8 7 6 5 4 3 2 1

Library of Congress Cataloging-in-Publication Data

Carle, Eric.

Have you seen my cat? / Eric Carle. — 1st Simon Spotlight ready-to-read ed.

p. cm. — (Ready-to-read)

Summary: A young boy encounters all sorts of cats while searching for the one he lost.

ISBN 978-1-4424-4574-1 (pbk.) — ISBN 978-1-4424-4575-8 (hardcover)

[1. Cats—Fiction.] I. Title.

PZ7.C21476Hav 2012

[E]—dc23

2011025830

Have you seen my cat?

This is not <u>my</u> cat!

Have you seen my cat?

This is not <u>my</u> cat!

Have you seen my cat?

This is not <u>my</u> cat!

Have you seen my cat?

This is not <u>my</u> cat!

Have you seen my cat?

This is not <u>my</u> cat!

Have you seen my cat?

This is not <u>my</u> cat!

Have you seen my cat?

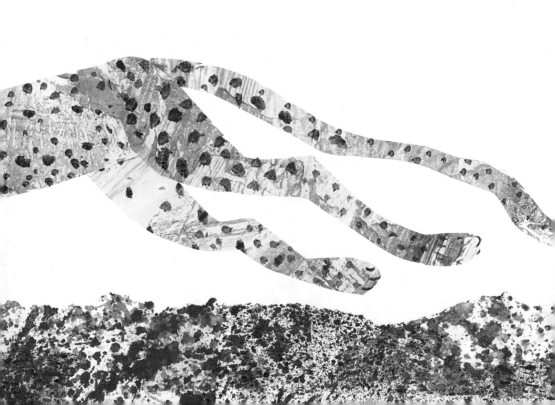

This is not m̲y̲ cat!

Have you seen my cat?

This is not <u>my</u> cat!

Where is my cat?

Have you seen my cat?

This is my cat!

Lion

Puma

Panther

Persian

Jaguar

Tiger

Bobcat

Cheetah